COIN TOSS

ADAPTED BY MARK S. BERNTHAL

SCHOLASTIC INC.

NEW YORK   TORONTO   LONDON   AUCKLAND   SYDNEY

MEXICO CITY   NEW DELHI   HONG KONG   BUENOS AIRES

No part of this publication may be reproduced in whole or in part, or stored in a retrieval system, or transmitted in any form or by any means, electronic, mechanical, photocopying, recording, or otherwise, without written permission of the publisher. For information regarding permission, write to Scholastic Inc., Attention: Permissions Department, 557 Broadway, New York, NY 10012.

ISBN 0-439-73383-9

Duel Masters, the Duel Masters logo, and characters' distinctive likenesses are trademarks of Wizards/Shogakukan/Mitsui-Kids. ©2005 Wizards/Shogakukan/Mitsui-Kids/ShoPro. Wizards of the Coast and its logo are trademarks of Wizards of the Coast, Inc.

HASBRO and its logo are trademarks of Hasbro and are used with permission. All Rights Reserved.

Published by Scholastic Inc.
SCHOLASTIC and associated logos are trademarks and/or registered trademarks of Scholastic Inc.

12 11 10 9 8 7 6 5 4 3 2 1   5 6 7 8 9/0

Printed in the U.S.A.
First printing, August 2005

INTRODUCTION

The world as we know it isn't the world around us. There are awesome creatures living in five mysterious civilizations, realms of Light, Water, Darkness, Fire, and Nature. They can be brought into our world through an incredible card game — Duel Masters!

Though many kids and adults play this game, only the best can call forth these creatures. They are known as *Kaijudo Masters*.

This is the story of one junior duelist unique among all others. His name is Shobu Kirifuda.

Y our prospect has done well," said the Master. His voice echoed eerily off the Temple's cold stone walls.

"He's still a bit arrogant," Knight responded, "but improving daily."

"When will you bring him here?" asked the Master.

Knight's dark sunglasses couldn't hide his uneasy expression. "I don't believe that is the route he should take. Despite what he thinks, he's still not ready to face Hakuoh."

"You show far too much caution," said the Master, waving a chalky white hand. "I believe he's more than ready for a real challenge."

Knight stood firm. "If you wish to proceed that way, I will have no part in it."

A grim smile crossed the Master's curled lips. "Your participation is no longer necessary."

"Master, please —" Knight urged.

"That will be all," ordered the dark leader.

Knight wheeled and left the room, his jaw tightly clenched.

Rekuta, Sayuki, and Mimi looked around the duelist training center with awe. "Wow!" exclaimed Rekuta. "This place is really big."

Shobu also gazed around, but he wasn't admiring the facility. He sought an opponent — a very special opponent.

Then Knight's familiar voice interrupted his search. "Glad you could make it. Let me show you around."

As Knight led the kids through the training center, they passed hundreds of young competitors. "The purpose of this facility is twofold," he explained. "First, we train young players to be world-class duelists. Second, we use dueling to bring young people from all over the globe together. We hope to promote understanding and world peace through this."

Peace was the last thing on Shobu's mind. He ignored all the faces he saw, continuing to seek one in particular.

"What's wrong, Shobu?" Knight inquired.

"Hakuoh is here, isn't he?" Shobu responded, his eyes darting around the room.

"Maybe," answered Knight calmly, "but Hakuoh is the top duelist in the world. He doesn't duel just anybody."

"Well, I'm not just anybody!" Shobu exclaimed, as he darted up the hall.

Knight rolled his eyes and calmly followed the dashing duelist, while signaling to the others to stay put.

Shobu blindly navigated a maze of hallways, shouting, "Hakuoh! Show yourself! I'll find you, so you'd

better get ready." At an intersection, he wheeled and walked backward, looking up another hall. "What do you think this is, hide-and-seek? Come out and face me, you *senpai!* It's about time you —"

A collision brought Shobu's rant to a sudden stop. He'd backed into a very solid person. When Shobu turned, he was shocked to spy the Master for the first time. Cloaked in a black robe, the Master seemed enormous. A hood covered his head as always and a shock of blond hair spilled down, hiding half of his face. But it took only the piercing gaze of his visible eye to stop Shobu dead in his tracks.

The Master sported a sinister sneer. "Well, Shobu Kirifuda. You're the spitting image of your father."

"Who . . . who are you?" Shobu inquired timidly.

"A friend. A friend who can lead you to Hakuoh," the Master answered quietly.

"Where is he?" Shobu asked.

"In a place where real players gather together to

become stronger," answered the cloaked one. "The Temple."

Shobu looked confused.

"This duel center alone won't help you improve your abilities," explained the Master. "Only the Temple has what you seek. We would be honored if you would join us." With that, he handed the young duelist a small card.

Just then, Shobu was distracted by Knight calling him. When he turned back, the Master was mysteriously missing.

"And then this guy in a dark robe invited me to the Temple!" Shobu exclaimed to his friends and Knight in the training center snack shop.

"Trust me," Knight replied, "you are not ready for that."

"I'm going to find Hakuoh, and you can't stop me," Shobu protested.

"It's dangerous," said Knight.

"Dangerous?" Rekuta muttered with a nervous gulp. "How?"

"I'm forbidden to tell you," Knight answered, "but

if I could, I'd say the beds are lumpy, their buffet is loaded with carbs, and there's a deep, dark, evil secret I can't reveal, because it would crush the spirit of every card player in the world."

"With that last one, we have a winner!" Sayuki exclaimed.

"Spare me the drama!" Shobu grumbled, shaking his head. "I'm going. I'll find and challenge Hakuoh. And then I'll prove who's best."

4

Shobu raced away from the duel center, tightly gripping the card the Master gave him. As he ran, he chanted, "Own the zone! Beat Hakuoh! Own the zone! Beat Hakuoh!" But suddenly his focus was interrupted by calls from behind him.

"Wait up, Shobu!"

"Yeah, slow down."

"Chill out a sec!"

He turned to find his friends Rekuta, Sayuki, and Mimi chasing him.

"You weren't trying to ditch your friends by any chance, were you?" Sayuki blurted sarcastically.

"Yeah," Mimi added, while catching her breath. "If you're going to the Temple, we're coming with you."

Rekuta patted his ever-present laptop duelist's database. "You might need our help."

"You heard Knight," Shobu answered. "This place could be dangerous."

"Then we'll share the danger," said Mimi, with uncharacteristic bravery. "Sorry, man, but you're stuck with us."

Shobu sighed. "All right, but hurry up. I want to take down Hakuoh today!"

They followed the route to the Temple printed on the card, and were passing though a heavily wooded part of town when the Temple finally came into view. The vines growing over its large stone walls gave it the look of a spooky old Aztec temple. But Shobu was too focused to be frightened. He quickly dashed toward the front entrance with the others hot on his heels.

Suddenly their path was blocked by a very unusual obstacle — what appeared to be a large rodent with horizontal ears, wearing a purple robe and matching hat! "Hello. What do you want?" he inquired.

"Hey, a talking squirrel," Rekuta shouted. "Dig those ears."

"He's cute!" said Sayuki.

"I love his outfit!" purred Mimi.

They all chuckled till the strange doorman shouted, "For your information, I am not a squirrel! I am Fritz, the bitter goblin. I guard the Temple and love karaoke."

"Karaoke?" Shobu muttered with surprise. "That's for people who can't sing."

"I'll have you know, karaoke is a legitimate art form," snapped the bitter goblin.

"Sure it is!" Shobu joked. "In a bizarre alternate universe called . . ."

"Nerd-Land!" shouted Rekuta, finishing the sentence.

Fritz studied Rekuta and replied, "Oh, I'm sure you're well acquainted with Nerd-Land, Small Fry."

Sayuki laughed. "He's got you there, Rekuta."

"Why don't we skip all this chatter about my singing and cut to the chase," said Fritz. "What are you doing here?"

Shobu held out the small card he'd been given. "The Master invited me, and I'm here to nuke Hakuoh."

Fritz smiled. "Wish I had a buck for every kid who said that. I'd be a rich little bitter goblin."

"Shobu is the winner of the Battle Arena Tournament," Rekuta blurted, defending his friend. "He's not afraid."

"Yeah! He's earned the right to duel inside the Temple," Sayuki added.

"This isn't the training center," Fritz replied. "The stakes are much higher here, and so are the consequences. Are you ready to take a little entrance exam?"

5

"Give me any question you can dream up, Stumpy!" Shobu declared with confidence.

"As long as it's about dueling," Sayuki whispered to Rekuta. "He's history if it's school stuff!"

Fritz forged ahead. "First question — when you pull cards from your shield zone, this trigger allows you play them without paying the cost. What's this trigger called?"

"A shield trigger," said Shobu, rolling his eyes. "How about something that makes me think?"

"Second question," Fritz continued. "Super Explosive Volcanodon —"

Shobu interrupted mid-question. "That's easy! Volcanodon has a power of 2,000 and when it attacks, its power triples to 6,000."

"Maybe," said Fritz, coolly, "but what if Volcanodon attacks Gigagiele, a slayer with a power of 3,000?"

Shobu thought a moment, and then smiled. "Tricky question, Squirrel Face! Volcanodon would win the battle, but would also be destroyed, thanks to Gigagiele's slayer ability."

The goblin nodded. "You're not as lame as that hair makes you look, kid."

Rekuta pumped his fist at Shobu's success. "Yes!"

Fritz didn't skip the chance to diss. "Don't slip into your cheerleading skirt yet, Stumpy."

Mimi's eyes popped. Then she whispered to Sayuki. "Maybe he saw Rekuta at the tournament."

"Listen carefully to the final question," said Fritz. "Your opponent has four copies of Hanusa, Radiance Elemental in the battle zone, and you have plenty of Fire Civilization and Darkness Civilization mana. How can you destroy all of your opponent's creatures during this turn by using only three creatures in your hand?"

Shobu frowned, thinking the question through. Then he turned to Rekuta. "Do you have a Darkness deck?"

"Dumb question, Shobu. You know my dad's the 'Supplier to the Dueling Stars.'" He immediately handed over the requested deck.

Shobu spread the cards on the ground, studying them and mumbling to himself. "To destroy four creatures with three cards, one card has to destroy two Hanusas.

But in the base set . . . there's no such card." Suddenly he brightened. "Wait! Terror Pit will do it!"

"No, it won't!" Rekuta shouted. "Terror Pit is a spell card! Maybe you should . . ."

"Cool it!" Shobu shouted. "Let me figure this out!"

"No. You cool it, Shobu!" exclaimed Sayuki. "We're friends trying to help. If this is what the Temple does to people, I don't like it."

"I'm sorry," said Shobu. "I didn't ask you guys to come along in the first place because I wanted to do this alone."

"You have thirty seconds to get into the Temple, smart guy. Better focus or Hakuoh's going to be a chuckling champion for a long time."

"Swamp Worm! That's it!" Rekuta shouted. "When you place him in the battle zone, your opponent has to choose one of his creatures to go to the graveyard! Use Swamp Worm and you'll be able to defeat Hanusa. It's perfect!"

"Won't work," said Shobu, shaking his head, "because I can only use the three cards in my hand. Even with Swamp Worm, I could only destroy three Hanusas. There has to be another angle."

"Ticktock," said Fritz, with a growing smirk. "Looks like you're just another duelist dud who will fall with a thud."

As the final seconds ticked away, Shobu frantically thought out loud, "If I can take a creature out of the battle zone and put it back in my hand, I'll have a chance! But only Water Civilization cards like Unicorn Fish and Saucerhead Shark can do that . . ." Then the answer hit him. "That's it! Re-use a card! I forgot all about that!"

He turned to Fritz at the last moment. "Okay, goblindygook, listen up! Here's the answer: First, I summon Rothus, the Traveler! Rothus has the ability to force each player to choose one creature from the

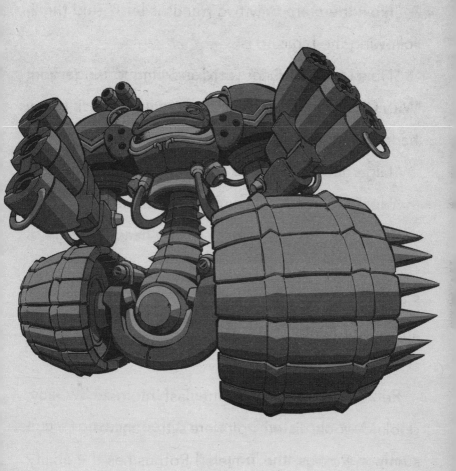

battle zone and send it to the graveyard! Then I can do the same thing and summon a second Rothus."

"Now there are only two Hanusas left!" said Mimi, following the logic.

"Next I use a Darkness card and summon Gigargon! With Gigargon, I can bring two creatures back to my hand from the graveyard."

"Gigargon's the key to winning!" shouted Rekuta.

"Now I'm ready to summon two Rothuses. And your question is answered!" Shobu heaved a sigh of relief.

"We have a winner," declared Fritz. "You've earned the right to enter the Temple."

"We're in!" cheered Sayuki.

Fritz waved a goblin finger. "Not 'we,' Sweetie. 'He'! Only those who answer three questions correctly may enter the Temple."

With that, Fritz flipped a coin token to Shobu and headed for the door.

"What's this for?" Shobu asked, studying the token.

"I'll tell you inside," Fritz answered. "That is, if you're coming."

Shobu raced to catch up to the spunky goblin. His friends watched with worried expressions.

"Let us know what happens when you get back," shouted Sayuki.

Mimi watched quietly, squinting a bit. Then she mumbled to herself, "Be careful Shobu. The Temple has a way of changing people."

How did she know?

6

In a dark Temple room, Hakuoh practiced with his dueling deck. The Master watched Hakuoh's game-play carefully, noting tiny details that the *senpai* could improve, and making suggestions about extremely subtle strategy decisions.

A cloaked guard entered. "Sir," he quietly announced, "the kid with the funny hair has arrived. You requested to know when he had entered the Temple."

Hakuoh continued to turn cards and mumbled with a sigh, "Another one?"

The guard held out a pocket security monitor with Shobu's image on the screen.

"It's him," Hakuoh said.

"Yes," the Master confirmed, "Shobu Kirifuda. You're not nervous, are you?"

"Of course not," the champion murmured. "Why should I be nervous? My hair is just as silly."

7

Fritz led Shobu down wet, slippery stairs to a dark, dungeonlike level of the Temple.

Shobu looked around nervously. "Are you taking me to Hakuoh?"

"You have a lot to prove before that happens," the goofy goblin replied as they arrived at a large hall filled with many duelists. All competed with grim faces.

"Whoa! These dudes are intense," Shobu observed.

"This is nothing, my little friend, Showboat."

"It's Sho*bu!*"

"Whatever. You won't be here long enough for anyone to learn your name, anyway."

Fritz gestured to the duelists. "These are just beginners. You think you're the only one who believes he's good enough to beat Hakuoh? Now hang on to that token while I tell you the rules."

"I know how to duel," said Shobu.

"I'm talking about the *Temple* rules," said Fritz. "Challenge any duelist down here. If you win, the loser gives you a token. If you lose, you give your opponent a token."

Just then, a nearby contest ended, forcing the loser to hand over his last token. Fritz giggled like a merry maniac. "Oh, I love this part. Watch!"

Suddenly, two large, hooded guards grabbed the loser and dragged him away kicking and screaming. Shobu's jaw dropped.

Fritz smiled slyly and explained. "Lose all your tokens and you're expelled from the Temple. Permanently."

"B-b-but you only gave me one," Shobu stammered. "If I lose now, I'll never face Hakuoh."

Fritz smiled. "Better make sure you win your first match, pretty boy, or it's a quick bye-bye for you."

"When can I challenge Hakuoh?"

"Win 50 tokens and you can go upstairs," said the goblin.

"Well, Fritz," said Shobu, with a sigh, "I've never met a better bitter goblin than you, and I'd really love to stand here and chat all day, but I have a date with Hakuoh!"

Shobu turned and confidently walked over to the nearest idle duelist, challenging him with a firm, "*Kettou da!*"

Fritz nodded. "A challenge has been made. Tokens will be exchanged. It is done."

Upstairs, the Master and Hakuoh observed all this on a closed-circuit TV. "Destiny has brought us together," said Hakuoh, studying Shobu in the monitor. "I'm waiting for you, Kirifuda. Let's see how good you really are."

The end was near and Shobu knew it. "Well, Dave, I'm going to bring out the big guns. *Ike!* Bolshack Dragon! Attack!"

Shobu's opponent slumped in defeat. "Someone stick a fork in Dave," said Shobu to some nearby spectators, "I think he's done."

Dave didn't get far from the table before being reminded of a slight technicality. "Ah . . . slow down there, Davey Boy. My compensation, please?" The loser grudgingly flipped a token to Shobu.

"Thank you, come again!" said Shobu, counting his tokens. "That makes sixteen. Thirty-four more and I'm dueling Hakuoh!" Then he dashed around the room, seeking his next victim. "Want to duel? Huh? Do you? Anybody? How about you?"

Hakuoh and the Master continued to follow Shobu's progress through hidden cameras. "It appears Kirifuda will have his fifty tokens — and a match with me — in no time," said Hakuoh.

"Maybe if he was dueling his little pals in the schoolyard," replied the Master, with a sly grin. "But here in the Temple, the rules are quite different." Then he turned back to view a close-up of Shobu's determined expression. Barely suppressing an evil laugh, the Master muttered, "Enjoy your last fleeting moments of success, Kirifuda!"

9

Rekuta's polka-dot bow tie wasn't very good camouflage, but the bushes were as thick as his glasses, so the Master's guards didn't see him checking out the Temple from a distance. He ducked down to consult with Sayuki and Mimi. "Doesn't look like we can sneak in the front door. Those hooded guards make Fritz look like a cheerful chipmunk."

"And you're sure Shobu only needs ten more tokens?" Sayuki asked.

"He called my dad's shop last night with the news," Rekuta replied. "Said he nuked everyone he'd played yesterday and was going to sleep over in the Temple's Duelist Dormitory. If we don't sneak in there some-how today, we'll miss his big duel with Hakuoh."

Sayuki batted her eyes and sighed. "Hakuoh is so dreamy."

Mimi's expression disagreed. "Beating Hakuoh won't be as easy as Shobu thinks," she muttered. "The Temple has many secrets."

"What did you say?" Rekuta asked.

Mimi shook her head. "Uh . . . nothing! Let's sneak around back and see if we can find a way in there."

As the kids crept through the bushes, Mimi thought, *Memo to me. Stop thinking out loud!*

10

Hakuoh was crushed! Devastated! Shobu raised his arms in conquest, feeling the thrill of total triumph wash over him. Every duelist and guard in the Temple cheered. Even Fritz was shouting.

"Wake up, Drool Master! You've missed breakfast!"

Shobu sat up sharply in bed, snapped from his wonderful dream. He got dressed and rushed to the dueling hall to resume his climb to a face-off with Hakuoh. He needed just ten more tokens from the lame dungeon duelists and he'd march upstairs to prove who was best!

But Shobu arrived to a very different sight than the day before. Every duelist in the room was waiting for him! And every face showed sly confidence. What had caused such a sudden change overnight?

Mimi crept carefully behind the Temple. She'd sent Rekuta and Sayuki in a different direction so she could be alone for a moment. Patting the stone wall, she muttered to herself, "This is going to ruin my manicure." She closed her eyes and concentrated for a minute. Then, glancing around to ~~be~~ sure no one could see her, she slowly raised both arms and brought them down in a circular motion. All senses focused, she struck the wall with a kung fu punch, shouting, "*Tasogare!* Blaze punch! *Hiyaaa!*"

and let Shobu and all those kids be destroyed? Can you be that evil?"

The kids' eyes bugged out like flying saucers when they heard that! But they couldn't stop listening. The debate continued as they listened with their ears pressed to the door.

"The Temple was established to find the best duelist," said the Master. "If Kirifuda's son is that person, you have nothing to worry about."

"The Temple was established to make sure Hakuoh stays at the top," Knight shouted.

The Master remained calm. "That's your interpretation. I see it as merely securing the future of dueling."

Just then, Shobu's friends heard a guard approaching. As they dashed away, Sayuki exclaimed, "Do you think the Master was serious?"

"Earth to Sayuki!" Rekuta answered. "I wouldn't doubt anything that hooded sleazeball says."

As they rounded the corner, the fleeing threesome stopped dead in their tracks. A shocking sight met their astonished gaze. Shobu sat on the floor with his back against the stone wall. He stared into space, babbling nonsense. "Welcome to Graceland, ladies and gentlemen, but Elvis has left the building."

"Shobu! Snap out of it!" Rekuta shouted, slapping his friend's cheeks.

But Shobu continued to mumble. "Want fizz in a whiz? Drink Gagalot Cola!"

"He's delirious," said Mimi, "but why?"

An unfamiliar voice responded, "Because Mr. Lucky is losing . . . big time!"

Shobu's friends looked up to find a group of duelists sporting smiles that screamed 'revenge!'

"He was undefeated yesterday," said another duelist, "but we've blown so many holes in him today, he's Swiss cheese."

Shobu's few remaining tokens were on the floor

next to him. A third duelist picked one up. "Wonder Boy forgot to pay me for drubbing him just now. He doesn't take defeat very well."

All strolled away, laughing and arguing over who would challenge Shobu next — if he ever regained his senses!

12

Mimi, Rekuta, and Sayuki wanted answers, and quickly, but they never expected to find them taped to a wall in a nearby room! Large sheets listed all the cards in Shobu's deck.

Rekuta paged through a notebook that was lying on the floor. "They've analyzed Shobu's dueling history," he gasped, "plus ways to beat him!"

Sayuki shook her head. "He'll never duel Hakuoh if they win all his tokens!"

Just then, Fritz entered, merging smoothly into the conversation. "It happens all the time around here.

Once a duelist starts flashing tokens, people notice. It doesn't take long before they figure out what's making him win."

Then he returned to his business. "Are you going to leave? Or do I have to call the guards?"

Mimi folded her arms defiantly. "We haven't seen the gift shop yet. We'd like to stay."

Fritz's eyes popped open as he realized something. Pointing at Mimi, he shook slightly and stuttered, "W-w-wait a minute! I know you. You're . . ."

"I'm no one, Fritz," Mimi interrupted. "Just a girl who wants some answers, and you're going to give them to me."

"I can't tell you anything," said Fritz. "I swear! I'm just a squirrel trying to earn a nut."

"I didn't think you were a goblin," said Sayuki, shaking her head.

Mimi stayed focused. "Tell us. Is this whole Temple thing just a scam to keep Hakuoh on top?"

"And does Hakuoh know what's going on here?" added Sayuki. "I hope not, because he's really dreamy."

"I . . . I'll have to plead the Fifth on that," stammered Fritz.

"You don't get off that easy," said Rekuta. "Come on, Super Squirrel, spill it."

Before Fritz could reveal any Temple mysteries, he was interrupted by a familiar voice. "I don't care about the Temple's goals."

Everyone turned, surprised to find Shobu standing in the doorway. He seemed much different: clearheaded and ready for battle.

"All I know is that if I want to duel Hakuoh, I need 50 tokens. That's why I came here. And I'm not giving up."

"You mean you're still going to duel?" asked Fritz in disbelief.

"Well, I didn't hang around for the breakfast buffet!" Shobu answered.

Though happy to see Shobu recover from his dueling doldrums, his pals were still concerned. Rekuta pointed to the charts on the wall. "They've already analyzed your deck, Shobu. You don't have a snowball's chance in a microwave of winning!"

"I still have three tokens," said Shobu. "Only 47 more to go."

Shobu wheeled and headed back for the dueling hall. Mimi shook her head and muttered, "He's going to need a lot more than confidence."

13

"Crystal Lancer! *Ike!*" shouted the victor. "And now for the final blow . . . *Todome da!*"

The defeated duelist grunted and slumped as he tossed a token across the table. That loser was Shobu. He was quickly back where he started the day before, holding only one token in his hand.

"You were right, Mimi," Rekuta observed, as he typed the final move into his computer. "Confidence alone hasn't cut it for Shobu."

"He's never gonna win with that deck," said Mimi.

Fritz completely abandoned his enforcer role and

observed the match with the kids. "He has one big problem. No Evolution creatures in his deck."

"Well, why doesn't he add some?" Sayuki asked.

"Shobu's never wanted to change the structure of his deck," said Rekuta.

Mimi looked surprised. "Why?"

"It's the deck his father gave him, and his father is the greatest Kaijudo master in the world. That deck's got sentimental value."

While many opponents argued over who would take Shobu's last token, he stared at his deck, looking crushed again. Just then, Mimi bumped into him. Cards from both their decks scattered everywhere as they fell to the ground.

"Oh my goodness!" said Mimi. "Your cards got mixed up with mine! Can you imagine? I am such a butterfingers."

Shobu's expression revealed his bad day was getting worse.

"Sorry," said Mimi. "But don't worry; your deck is all Fire Civilization cards, so I'll just pick them up for you!" She quickly gathered cards off the floor and handed them to Shobu. "Here you go! Your deck! No one else's!"

Shobu checked the deck carefully. "Hey, wait!" he exclaimed, holding some cards up. "These aren't mine! You know I don't have any Evolution creatures!"

Mimi's little trick was discovered, but she decided to keep at it anyway. She leaned over to Shobu and whispered, "Your deck has no Evolution cards because they didn't exist when your father left."

Shobu nodded quietly.

"But since he's a Kaijudo Master," Mimi continued, "he's probably changed with the times and built a great deck using them now. He'd advise you to do the same, don't you think?"

Shobu remained silent. As he stared at the cards thoughtfully, a cocky duelist, who called himself Attack Dog, approached with a sneer. "Don't look so sad, Kirifuda," he taunted. "I'm about to put you out of your misery. I just won the coin toss, and have the honor of taking your last token!"

14

Despite the crowd surrounding the table, the hall was silent. It appeared Attack Dog would permanently banish Shobu from the Temple!

"And now for your listening pleasure," Attack Dog boasted to the spectators, "I'd like to perform a symphony of broken shields!"

Rekuta typed the move into his computer and muttered, "Attack Dog's whipping Shobu. He's doomed!"

"Guess he decided not to change his deck," said Mimi.

Attack Dog drew their attention back to the table,

bragging, "You know, Kirifuda, this may be the quickest defeat in dueling history. Somebody alert the medics."

Shobu debated his next move, while Attack Dog continued his rant. "What will the amazing Shobu will play next? I'm guessing Brawler Zyler."

Sure enough, Shobu played Brawler Zyler.

"I told you!" Attack Dog bragged, "Guess I just have a sixth sense about these things. Or could it be we've all memorized your deck, Kirifuda?"

Shobu calmly smiled for the first time that day. "But here's another card, just for good measure. Attack Puppy, meet Armored Blaster Valdios!"

"W-what?" stammered Attack Dog. "Y-you don't have that . . ."

"I do now," answered Shobu. "Valdios, attack! *Ike!* Finish him — *Todome da!*"

Attack Dog and the other basement duelists were

in total shock. Even Shobu's friends were a little blown away!

"Shobu won!" shouted Sayuki.

"He changed his deck after all," Mimi observed with a smile.

"Yep," said Shobu, joining them. "Thanks, Mimi. I was so attached to my dad's deck that I lost sight of the real goal — to be the best duelist. And if that means changing my cards now and then, you better believe that's what I'm going to do! I came here on a mission, and now I'm going to finish it."

With that, he turned to the gawking duelists. "I believe there was a line forming to challenge me," he said. "Which one of you deckers is next? The only coin toss you'll be part of from now on is when you're flipping a token to me!"

15

"... 47 ... 48 ... 49 ... and 50!" Shobu finished counting out his tokens to Fritz. Fifty dazed duelists surrounded them, all looking like they'd been hit by a truck.

"Shobu's new deck is so cool," said Mimi.

"Going upstairs is so cool," added Rekuta.

"Seeing Hakuoh upstairs is so cool," purred Sayuki.

"I never thought you'd win 49 straight matches with that new deck," said Fritz, "but here's what you've been waiting for." The super squirrel handed

Shobu a key. "This will let you into the Temple's big leagues, kid. Good luck!"

As his friends cheered, Shobu held the key high. "Watch out, Hakuoh! I've got a new deck and a new attitude. And I'm unstoppable!"

DuelMasters

D-MAX Membership Offer

Join **D-MAX**--the official Duel Masters fan club-- and get previews, updates and loads of cool stuff!

Follow these 4 steps to become a D–MAX member.

Important! If you are under 13, one of your parents will need to sign this form.
If your parent does not sign the form, we won't be able to enroll you in D-MAX.

1) Read this. By filling out this form you are enrolling in the **D-MAX** program. This will make you eligible for promotional mailings, email updates, contests, and other programs.

2) Give us your contact information.

First Name _____ Last Name _____

Address _____ Birth date _____

City _____ State/Province _____

Country* (check one): ☐ U.S.A.   ☐ Canada _____

ZIP/Postal Code

Phone _____ Email _____

* Offer only valid in the U.S. and Canada.
For other countries, go online at www.duelmasters.com and download your local application form.

3) Get your parents to sign this form after reading the "Parents" information if you are under 13.

Parent/Guardian's Printed Name _____

Parent/Guardian's Signature _____

4) Put this form into a stamped envelope and send it to:
D-MAX
Wizards of the Coast
P.O. Box 1080
Renton WA 98057

Limit one D-MAX membership per person. "Free stuff" offer only available while supplies last. Allow 6-8 weeks for delivery.

PARENTS: Your child would like to register for the D-MAX program from Wizards of the Coast. When you send in this form, he will be sent a membership kit including fun printed materials related to Duel Masters and a membership card. From time to time he may also be sent other physical mailings and emails. In addition, he will gain access to a special area of the Duel Masters web site.

While visiting the Duel Masters web site, your child may change his contact information and participate in online surveys. Before we can allow your child's personal and demographic information to be viewed and modified online, we want to notify you about our online information collection practices and obtain your permission. We ask you first read through the "Note to Parents" in the Wizards Website Privacy Statement (http://www.wizards.com/parents), which identifies the personal information that Wizards of the Coast collects from children online and the way we handle such information. If you cannot connect to our web site, our customer service team can provide you with the information and answer any other questions (800-424-6496).

When you have finished and wish to provide your consent, please sign this registration form where it says "Parent/Guardian's Signature."

Please note that once you have signed and sent us this form, you always have the ability to: (i.) review your child's personal information collected online; (ii.) request that we delete your child's personal information online; (iii.) stop us from further using or collecting additional personal information online about your child without gaining new permission from you. To do so, please contact us using the information provided above.

DMSCUS

Go online for more details at
WWW.DUELMASTERS.COM